A BOY, A DOG, A FROG and A FRIEND

by Mercer

and Marianna Mayer

Millersburg Elementary

Library

Dial Books for Young Readers
New York

Copyright © 1971 by Mercer and Marianna Mayer. All rights reserved.
Library of Congress Catalog Card Number: 70-134857
First Pied Piper Printing 1978
Printed in Hong Kong by South China Printing Co.
C O B E
4 6 8 10 9 7 5
A Pied Piper Book is a registered trademark of Dial Books for Young Readers
A division of E. P. Dutton | A division of New American Library
® TM 1,163,686 and ® TM 1,054,312
A BOY, A DOG, A FROG AND A FRIEND is published in a hardcover edition by
Dial Books for Young Readers, 2 Park Avenue, New York, New York 10016
ISBN 0-8037-0804-1

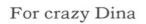
For crazy Dina